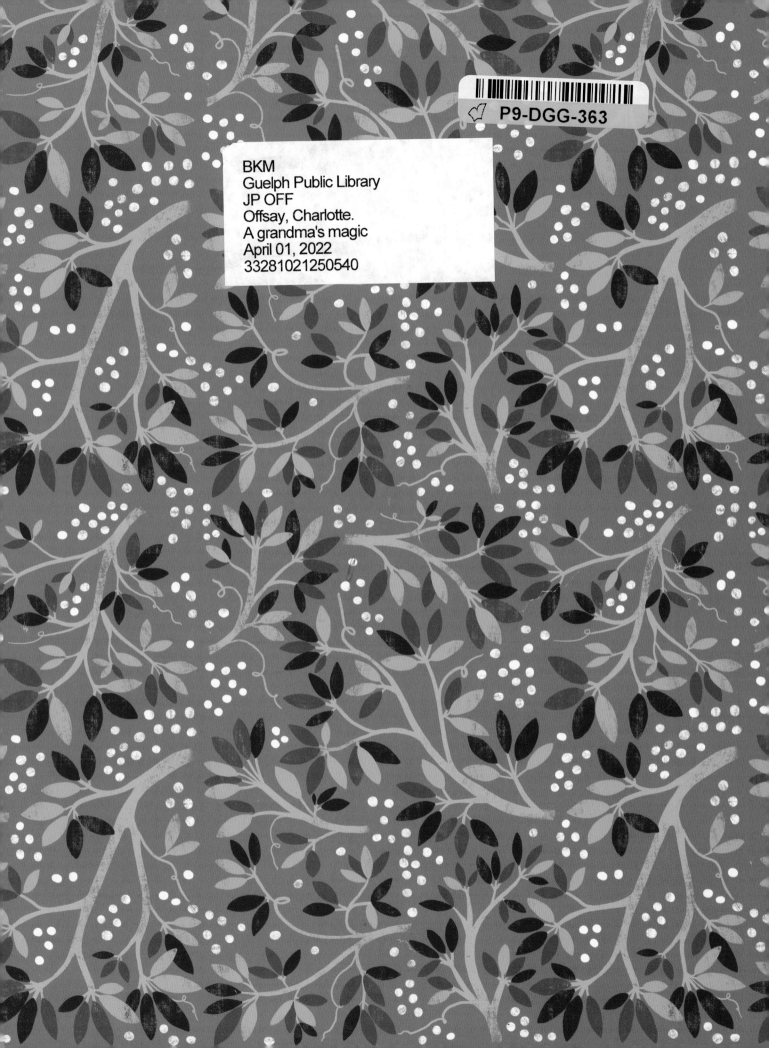

For Shirley Hold JP OFF ia, whose magic
turns th d golden

To Therese, for offering to be a
grandmother to my boys
—Å.G.

All rights reserved. Published in the United States by Doubleday, an imprint of Random House Children's Books, a division of Penguin Random House LLC, New York.

Doubleday and the colophon are registered trademarks of Penguin Random House LLC.

Visit us on the Web! rhcbooks.com

Educators and librarians, for a variety of teaching tools, visit us at RHTeachersLibrarians.com

Library of Congress Cataloging-in-Publication Data
Names: Offsay, Charlotte, author. | Gilland, Åsa, illustrator.
Title: A grandma's magic / by Charlotte Offsay ; illustrated by Åsa Gilland.
Description: First edition. | New York : Doubleday, [2022] | Audience: Ages 2–5. |
Summary: An illustrated celebration of grandmothers and the magic they perform as they
sweep children away on adventures, help create in the kitchen and garden, and turn worries into giggles.
Identifiers: LCCN 2020052278 (print) | LCCN 2020052279 (ebook) |
ISBN 978-0-593-37600-3 (hardcover) | ISBN 978-0-593-37601-0 (library binding) |
ISBN 978-0-593-37602-7 (ebook)
Subjects: CYAC: Grandmothers—Fiction. | Grandparent and child—Fiction.
Classification: LCC PZ7.1.O38 Gr 2022 (print) | LCC PZ7.1.O38 (ebook) | DDC [E]—dc23

MANUFACTURED IN CHINA
10 9 8 7 6 5 4 3 2 1
First Edition

Random House Children's Books supports the First Amendment and celebrates the right to read.

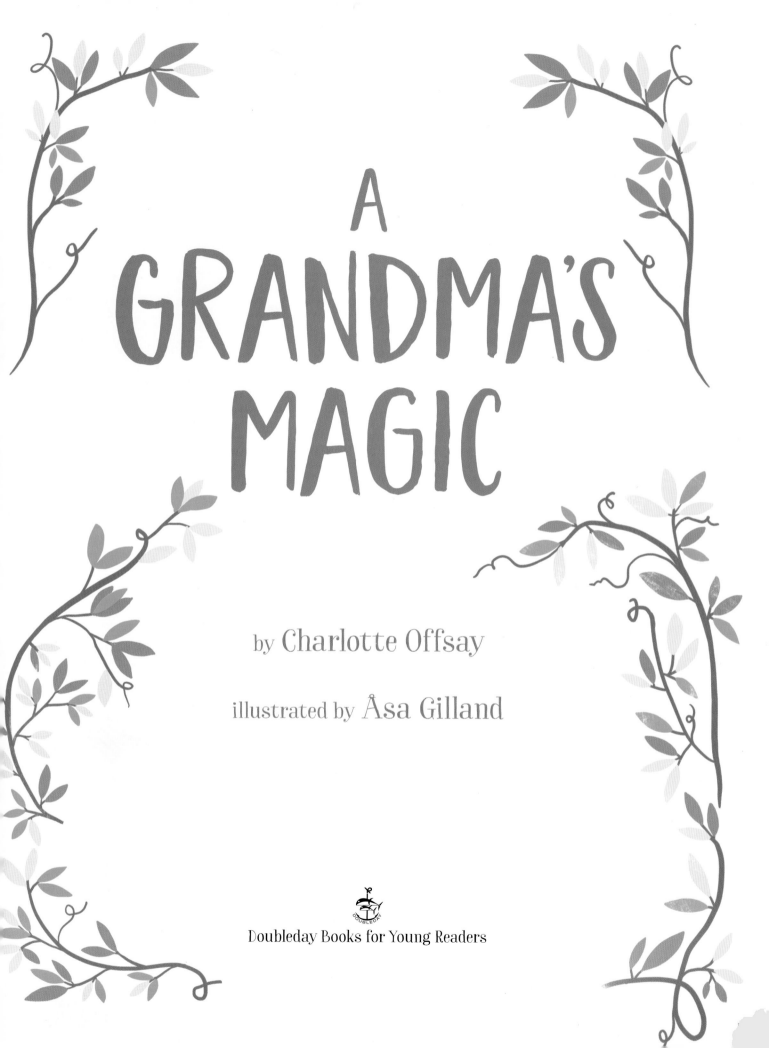

A
GRANDMA'S
MAGIC

by Charlotte Offsay

illustrated by Åsa Gilland

Doubleday Books for Young Readers

When a child is born . . .

. . . a grandma is born too.

Grandmas aren't like regular grown-ups.
Grandmas are filled with magic.

A grandma's magic bursts through the door,
scoops you up, and sweeps you away to adventure.

Together you conquer new heights,

uncover secret wonders,

and tame wild beasts.

A grandma's magic has no schedule.

It zooms.

It wanders.

There's nowhere else it would rather be.

Her magic swirls inside your creations.
Together you sing her apple crumble recipe
until the whole world is golden.

A grandma's magic dances through your hands,
digging, planting, waiting, discovering new beginnings.

Her magic loops and weaves,
transforming the simplest things into timeless treasure.

And when disaster strikes,
the fun has faded,
and it seems like too much for Grandma to fix . . .

. . . you discover even a grandma's touch is magic.
Her arms melt the hurt,
her fingers mend the impossible,
and her kisses turn belly worries into belly giggles.

But sometimes she has to pack up her
grandma things and head home.
It can be hard to let her go.

But don't worry.

Because the most magical thing about Grandma . . .

. . . is that her magic never leaves.
It stays with you,

always.